W9-AAW-181

This book belongs to:

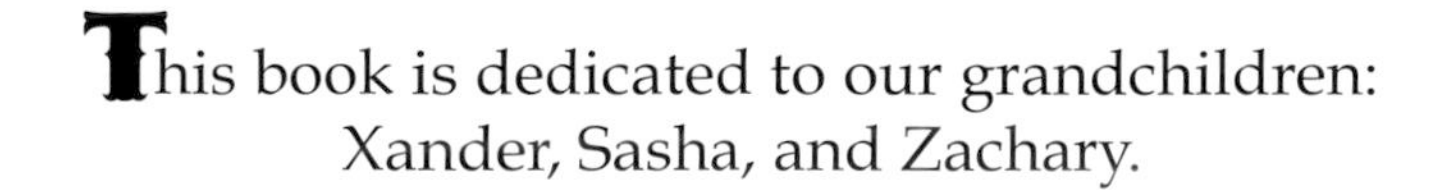

This book is dedicated to our grandchildren:
Xander, Sasha, and Zachary.

Reading with children is so important, and we loved sharing stories and reading with our own children. It is amazing to see what an impact the reading time made, especially the reading of great stories which so naturally imparted important life lessons.

The Land of Caring Bou was written with the desire to share a great story with our grandchildren. It is a story to help them learn that understanding and appreciating our differences ultimately brings us closer together. We share it with you, hoping you will read it, enjoy it, share it…and nurture greater understanding.

Michael and Donna Coles

Published 2006 by August House, Inc.
3500 Piedmont Road, Suite 310
Atlanta, Georgia 30305
404-442-4420

www.augusthouse.com

Book design by Timothy Banks
Art direction by Graham Anthony

Library of Congress Cataloging-in-Publication Data

Coles, Michael Joseph, 1944-
The land of Caring Bou / Michael & Donna Coles ; with Rob Cleveland & Ric Reitz ; illustrated by Timothy Banks.
p. cm.
Summary: When a herd of caribou abandons the forest after a devastating summer fire, it leaves behind a young hare, owl, bear, sheep, and duck who must learn to fend for themselves during the coming winter.
ISBN-13: 978-0-87483-814-5 (alk. paper)
ISBN-10: 0-87483-814-2 (alk. paper)
[1. Forest animals--Fiction. 2. Caribou--Fiction. 3. Self-reliance --Fiction.] I. Coles, Donna Jean, 1945- . II. Cleveland, Rob, 1955- . III. Reitz, Ric. IV. Banks, Timothy, ill. V. Title.
PZ7.C677135 2006
[E]--dc22 2006021125

Printed in Canada

written by **Michael and Donna COLES**

Co-written by **Rob CLEVELAND & Ric REITZ**

art by **Timothy BANKS**

AUGUST HOUSE

www.augusthouse.com

ATLANTA

The herd of Caring Bou was on the move. A season of snow was on its way and finding food would be harder than ever this year. A late summer forest fire had burned much of Caribou Pass.

The Caring Bou were always first to leave. When they heard the crunch of drying leaves and felt the growing chill of the mornings, they knew before the other animals that snow would soon cover the land.

Big Bou knew the herd would find plenty of food and shelter in the valley below. He knew most of his mountain kingdom would sleep under a snowy blanket and wake to a fresh spring. He even knew their forest would grow again, given a chance to rest.

Tagging along with the Caring Bou were the herd's newest members – a snowshoe hare, a snowy owl, a black bear, a bighorn sheep, and a clown duck. The Caring Bou had found them huddled together as fire swept through the forest and adopted them into the herd.

Big Bou knew the young ones should not move back and forth with the herd, but stay here in their natural home.

"I am very sorry," Big Bou began. "It is best for you to stay behind."

"No!" the bear growled. "What will we do without you?"

Big Bou thought hard. Then he said, "Follow me."

Big Bou led them to Peaceful Pond. He told them, "This will be your new home. It has all the food and shelter that you will need for the winter."

"When will you come baa-ck?" the sheep asked.

"When the snow turns to water," he replied. "Each of you has special gifts. Use them to protect Peaceful Pond and each other. Do not worry. I will not be far away."

Left alone, the young animals paced back and forth.

"We must protect Peaceful Pond," the hare said, just before tripping over his giant feet.

"Who?" cooed the owl. "Protecting Caribou Pass is the job of the Caring Bou."

"To be like Bou, we must do what Bou do," the duck quickly quacked.

Using twigs and vines
the youngsters made
antlers so they would
look more like Caring Bou.
Standing tightly together,
they were now ready
for the winter.

Big Bou
watched from
behind a cluster of trees.
He giggled at the sight of
their antlers. While he did not
like leaving the young animals,
he knew they would be alright.

As the wind blew colder and the snowflakes began to fall, the little group knew they were supposed to do something. But what would a herd of Caring Bou really do?

The youngsters looked
at the falling snow.

"We should warn all of
the other animals about the
coming storm," said the sheep.

"You are right," growled
the bear. "That is what the
Caring Bou would do!"

The clown duck laughed out loud as she watched the others, until she attempted to swim... and just sank. Seeing her stuck at the bottom of the pond, a school of fish got the last laugh.

Big Bou had seen enough. He gathered the struggling youngsters once more for a heart-to-heart talk.

"I guess we will never be Bou," baaed the sheep.

The others had to agree.

"Look into the water,"
Big Bou urged.
"Do you know
what I see? I see
a hare, an owl,
a bear, a sheep and
a duck, each with
your own strengths."

“I see a lightning quick hare
who is even faster in snow.
You were made for winter.”

"I see an owl who can soar high, both night and day, and is blessed with very special sight. You will find animals in Caribou Pass that others might miss."

"I see a bear who is strong enough to build a bridge or rescue anyone in need."

"I see a sheep that is able to climb the steepest slopes to reach out-of-the-way places."

"What about me?"
asked the clown duck.
Big Bou paused before
answering, "I see a duck
who swiftly swims."
"And?"
"And warns his
watery friends."
"Yes!"

"You already are part of our Caring Bou family and you just need to be you," Big Bou finished.

The little ones looked at one another and then slowly removed their wooden antlers. Big Bou was right.

When the snow finally turned back to water, the Caring Bou did return just as Big Bou had promised. The slightly older, but much wiser hare, owl, bear, sheep and duck greeted the herd. They had done what was asked of them, and Big Bou was very proud.

Spring was in the air. The mountain forest was showing signs of new life. The Caring Bou family was back together. And everything in Caribou Pass was as it should be.